The Dreaded Sunshine

Tyler Williams

PAGE PUBLISHING
Conneaut Lake, PA

First originally published by Page Publishing 2024

ISBN 979-8-89315-987-5 (pbk)
ISBN 979-8-89315-998-1 (digital)

Printed in the United States of America

Prologue

ON THE TENTH OF JANUARY IN 2179, a meteorite crashes on the border of the Democratic Republic of Akamot and the Kingdom of Rosellon. The crater it leaves is one hundred meters in diameter and fifteen meters in depth. The substance the rock is made of is unknown to the periodic table. Krydium, as it has come to be known, had outstanding capabilities. In its uncorrupted state, it could be used as a cure for ailments, a method to heal wounds and scars, and a reliable power source.

Seeing the potential capital gain from having complete control of this substance, King Ito of Rosellon launches an incursion into Akamot on the third of March to establish a monopoly on krydium. Queen Ryoko, who was an accomplished general in the army before marrying the king, advises him to abide by the agreement he signed with Chairman Tokala Hatahali to share this valuable resource and avoid the risk of losing it all. Prime Minister Toshiki Ichimada, Ito's brother, convinces him to take the grave risk and launch the incursion. The king believed it would be a sure success since he was personally leading this assault on Akamot's sovereignty. Unfortunately for His Majesty, Chairman Tokala expertly anticipated his greed, and so he would instead pay for his arrogance with his pride and his crown on the twenty-eighth of August 2179.

Crown Princess Rika, firstborn daughter of King Ito and Queen Ryoko, watches on helplessly as the throne she was to inherit vanishes. She sits at the dinner table for what she knows will be her last time residing in the Great Royal Palace. Clutching her knife with fury and frustration, she curses her father's cowardice while vowing to take back everything that is hers. Her anger turns to confusion as she feels the knife in her right hand has turned into a thick silver goo. Just when her mother enters the dinner hall to witness the abnormal event, the silver goo turns into a strong combat knife.

There is a strange bright-white glow in Rika's eyes, around her body, and the heart-shaped necklace her mother bought for her seventeenth birthday two weeks prior. Standing bewildered, she asks her mother where she got this odd jewel. Ryoko remembers she bought it from a jeweler who got the material directly from the krydium mines. After consulting the best doctors and scientists in the country to understand her daughter's condition, they tell her that krydium affects a person's DNA based on how they interact with their environment. The necklace made from the material gave Rika a strong form of telekinesis: the ability to manipulate matter.

She is now gifted with the power to change the molecular structure of an object, move it from a distance, and propel herself through the air. Ryoko Ichimada returns to her role as brigadier general after being able to secure a good position for her and her daughter with the help of her brother-in-law. The military training, support from her mother, extraordinary new ability, and her determination to achieve her goal has made it all clear as crystal to Rika. A wide devilish smile creeps across her face as she is now certain of her path ahead and how she will tread it.

C H A P T E R

1

A Soldier's Beginning

ON THE EIGHTEENTH OF MAY IN 2184, eighteen-year-old Aminata Keita is graduating from Diamondata Academy. After four years of eventful secondary education, she looks forward to a bright future. At the same time, she is trying to figure out what she will do that gives her a profound sense of purpose. As the daughter of the grand councilor of Rosellon, there is no scarcity of opportunity. Her father wants her to have a successful career primarily while her mother wants her to do what makes her happy more than anything else, and she is struggling to find a balance.

Just six years ago, when she and the rest of the Keita family were living in a simple working-class environment on the outskirts of the capital, she could never dream of such possibilities. Anything has become possible since the night the meteorite struck. The effect of krydium on daily life has been nothing short of impactful. Though the country failed to acquire control over krydium, 35 percent of the population of 355 million has been reported to be affected by it. As a krydian, Aminata knew this personally well. She has potential in ergokinesis, the ability to manipulate energy. Although she never really took much time to develop her power since she received it, she believes there is much she can do.

Her family is eager to support her in all her endeavors. Fatouma, her twenty-year-old sister, used her power of biokinesis in her prospects as a medical student. Her brother, Amadou, is a soldier who

1

can expertly control temperature well at the age of twenty-three. Her mother, Fadimata, could manipulate any plant life around her. Lastly, her father, Grand Councilor Adama Keita, had an ability that was unknown even to them. Because he went directly to the site of the meteorite when it crashed, they were all affected.

His Eminence the Grand Councilor is six months away from facing reelection against Morvolio Moretti to remain the country's head of state and government. A year after King Ito's abdication, he was elected as the leader of the State of Rosellon with overwhelming support from the nation's workers. Adama wants to celebrate his daughter's graduation at the newest restaurant in downtown Diamondata. Amadou and Fatouma think a simple celebration at the palace would be enough, but their mother insists on doing something special. Before they can even start heading there, Adama is engaged in a series of questions by the press.

As Adama speaks to them about the renegade forces, his daughter notices three individuals suspiciously moving into positions around the vicinity. Suddenly, the trio pull out hidden pistols to aim at the grand councilor. Before they can shoot, Aminata swiftly subdues them by shooting energy beams she channels through a pen. The three assailants are from the Army of the Phantom Sword, a renegade army that once functioned as a state-operated paramilitary.

Led by the former prime minister, Prince Toshiki Ichimada, the renegade army has utilized all manner of means to restore his leadership. When Adama defeated Toshiki to occupy the role that was reorganized from prime minister to grand councilor, the Army of the Phantom Sword remained loyal to him. As the loving brother of the deposed king, he proclaims Adama Keita to be illegitimate and has vowed to do whatever possible to end him. The prince also thinks he might have had something to do with the disappearance of the old king.

With the assailants subdued by the grand councilor's personal guard, an army officer arrives to assess the situation. She quickly takes notice of the heroism of the grand councilor's daughter, then offers her a chance to join the army of Rosellon. As an officer responsible for their company comprised of soldiers wielding gifted abilities,

Army Lieutenant Zynda Yamashita displays her ability to manipulate sound by using acoustic levitation on her glass of water. Aminata, with support from her parents, sees the offer as a chance to protect those she loves. Not one to let a good opportunity pass, she happily accepts the offer.

The Elite Strike Operation Force or Ark Strikers, comprised of krydian soldiers, gave Aminata the chance to channel her abilities and develop them in a way that would be effective in combating the likes of Phantom Sword. Within this section of the army is Unit 380. On the outskirts of Diamondata is the military base Aminata will train on for this very purpose. Being ambidextrous, she was given a pair of sickles resembling scythes specially made so that she could use to channel her power efficiently. What also helped her get accustomed to the rigorous training of a unit focused on superhuman abilities were her fellow soldiers within this unit.

Takara Shibata, who was also personally selected by Lieutenant Yamashita from the city of Violet View, can move with speed like no other when she uses her power over motion to accelerate her own. Her fastest recorded speed so far was 925 kilometers (about 574.77 miles) per hour. Her power came when she was trapped with twenty Phantom Sword renegades surrounding her in her hometown over four years ago. Standing in a cramped hiding place at her job where she had krydium near her for three weeks, she had her power awakened when all the motion around her ceased. She shares a common interest in punk metal with Aminata and helps her whenever she trains with kinetic energy.

Darion Benjamin Ellis, who worked as an engineer from the small town of Hollow Mine, could manipulate anything that had an electromagnetic current and generate his own electric energy. He received his ability when he accidentally shorted out his light before lighting it up again with his bare hand. His current threshold is 50,000 volts in permitting environments. His most common techniques are electromagnetic absorption, concentration, detection, and solidification. He is happy to help the newest comrade whenever she must train with electric energy.

Maxim "Ace" Vetrov, son of Security Council Secretary Ivan Vetrov and Viktoriya Vetrova from the town of Dreaton, wielded the ability to manipulate light. He worked as a lighting technician when his father brought him a piece of krydium to show off. His father inspired him to take part in the army and encouraged him to focus his skill with this power. Now a photokinetic soldier with a love of taking risks, he aims to make his father proud.

Jack Killdeer from the city of Swan Silver was looking to develop his skill in his power to grow minerals on his body. He could grow minerals such as granite and crystal on his body and use them for defense and offense. He felt he had to do his part for his country amid the Phantom Crisis. He got his powers when he was working with minerals when his colleague allowed him to take a piece of the precious new material with him. After keeping it with him for a week, a diamond grew out of his hand while drinking a glass of orange juice.

Tlalli Valiente could make the ground shake with her ability to manipulate damage. Before she became a soldier, she worked in construction. She attained her powers when a brand-new material was brought over from the site of the meteorite. She spent a week working near the krydium until she bent a steel beam without meaning to. Given a poleax to channel her power through, she has the chance to use her gift effectively.

Xochitl Valiente, Tlalli's younger sister, could bend any shadow to her will. She often preferred the comfort of shade as opposed to light and held a displease for sunny days. Tlalli would sometimes lend her sister clothing that had krydium residue on it. With umbrakinesis at her disposal and a scythe in hand, she strikes fear in the hearts of her enemies. The sisters believe it is necessary to lay down their lives against Phantom Sword after their father was killed in an attack by the renegade army.

The first task Aminata is to carry out on the orders of her company's fierce captain is to neutralize Mayor Quincy Vaughn of the coastal city of Swan Silver. The mayor's connection to Phantom Sword has been uncovered. With the state after him, Mayor Vaughn prepares a defense complete with his own soldiers. Aminata, Darion,

Jack, and Takara will be going on this mission under Lieutenant Yamashita's leadership while the others will stay at the base to ensure security at the capital. For the first time ever, Aminata will be using her powers for combat.

All civilians were evacuated from the city center before it could become a combat zone. Numerous Phantom Sword soldiers confront the army sent to apprehend Mayor Vaughn. This proved not only his corruption but his desperation as well. His previous attempts to bribe police officials only served to draw suspicion to his activities. He intends for the militants to hold off the army long enough for him to escape rather than defeat them.

The Ark Strikers, assisting the regular army troops, arrive to make sure that is impossible. The lieutenant uses her amazing power over sound to manipulate the enemy's perception of reality. Jack helps to shield his fellow soldiers while Darion uses his conduction technique to overcome flanking maneuvers by the enemy. Takara stops two squads of enemies by halting the motion of one squad long enough for them to be subdued and neutralizing the other herself with her speed. Lastly, the task of neutralizing the rogue mayor fell to Aminata.

Before he can take off in his vehicle, Aminata disables it with her energized twin sickles. A desperate Mayor Vaughn grabs a nearby grenade from one of his downed guards to throw it at Aminata. He runs away, only for her to deflect it back in his direction. The grenade explodes just far away enough so as to not kill the mayor. Though his injuries from the blast are serious, he is expected to survive to face trial for his seditious activity.

Having made it through her first mission, Aminata feels strong. She knows they are all here for the common goal of fighting for peace. Having risked life and limb alongside this band of gifted soldiers, she wholeheartedly believes she is one of them. It is astounding for her to have built a keen sense of comradery with a group of people she has known for only over a month. With the defeat of a major leader in the renegade army now building her reputation, her sights are set on Toshiki Ichimada.

Upon their return to the base, Aminata is praised by her comrades for directly putting an end to the actions of the rogue mayor. Lieutenant Zynda Yamashita laughs at how pathetic the now-deposed Vaughn's efforts to evade capture were. Upon hearing of the captain's upcoming visit, the proud lieutenant strongly insists on a direct training session with the captain. Corporal Keita is flattered at the idea of getting to spar with the captain herself but is also quite anxious. Ace, regarding Aminata's reward with envy, becomes shocked when the coin he flips keeps spinning in the air. It is then that the unit's attention is drawn to the front door. Standing there with an outstanding athletic build, long frost-white hair, a height of 184 centimeters, and a delightful smile is Army Captain Rika Ichimada.

Corporal Keita is surprised to be under the command of the heiress to the former throne. Sensing exciting potential, Captain Ichimada is eager to test her newest recruit's abilities firsthand after a successful operation. Aminata pushes herself to her limit, but the captain's expertise is overwhelming. Whether it was her training weapons or her bare hands, she could not lay a single scratch on her superior officer. Just as the fight appears to be won when Rika uses her ensnare technique to defeat her subordinate, Aminata instinctively breaks the telekinetic snare. This tires out Corporal Keita from sparring any longer.

Though this is defeat, the possibility of anyone physically challenging the great power the captain wielded was unheard of. This was a shock to everyone including Corporal Keita herself. Captain Ichimada becomes more pleased with the Ark Strikers and the selections made by her right-hand woman. The potential was so promising she had to take full advantage of the skill under her command. She intends to personally help Corporal Keita develop her power into something great for her cause and the country.

Before she can further discuss the matter, she is notified about the deposed rogue mayor's condition. Darion, Ace, Tlalli, and Takara personally commend their good friend on her sparring session with the captain and a successful mission. On their downtime, they celebrate the success on this day later that night at Ruby's Café. The five soldiers are enjoying themselves talking about their time in the army.

They all regard their first mission with Aminata with delight. Darion says, "You sure know how to make an impression."

Tlalli says as she encourages her comrade, "Don't be ashamed of losing to the captain. She's the toughest."

Ace says, "Even though she goes easy on us, we still lose." Hailed as the strongest krydian, Captain Ichimada is responsible for the country's 180 most powerful soldiers and has gained a reputation for testing her subordinates' abilities.

The rogue mayor's ambition to use the renegade paramilitary to take the Solton Prefecture and form his own breakaway state is revealed. Ace sarcastically exclaims, "All hail, King Quincy," when he jokes at such an ill-conceived plan. Tlalli believes if they keep dealing with renegade leaders as dumb as Vaughn, Toshiki will not be much of a problem for long. It is then that the report comes out that deposed mayor Quincy Vaughn of Swan Silver has succumbed to his injuries. With a major threat completely neutralized, their mission is a success.

This experience was unfathomably surreal for Aminata since she had never taken a life before. While Mayor Vaughn had by no means been a respectable man, she had to process ending someone's existence. Her friends try to lift her spirits by reminding her that the task of protecting those she cared for would likely come down to some heavy situations. Darion states that due to the volatile situation they faced, the loss of life was unfortunately bound to happen. After Takara emphasizes how deeply corrupt Vaughn was, Aminata feels a sense of ease knowing that awful man was no longer alive.

Takara and Darion then tell of their first experiences with taking a life. For Takara, it was when she hyper-accelerated her speed to stop a group of armed thieves. Though the mission was to subdue the attackers, Takara killed one by accident when she broke his neck. For Darion, it happened when he accidentally sent an electric shock that was more powerful than he wanted to an unsuspecting enemy. These instances demonstrated how the present situation took a lot of choice out of their hands.

As soldiers, they had to recognize that there would be actions they did not mean to take. Nothing will bring back a single life they ended. They must constantly remind themselves of the nature of their intentions and their goal. Whether they be ill-intentioned or not, they must be aware of who is opposing that goal. They must always remember this to avoid becoming heartless monsters and to never forget their collective role as protectors.

Twenty minutes before the news broke at Swan Silver General Hospital, a nurse moves the expired body of the rogue mayor to the morgue. After she relays her deed via phone, she is rewarded for carrying out her orders by Army Captain Rika Ichimada. Since Mayor Vaughn's personal ambition was incongruous with her plan, he had to be removed by whatever means possible. She is pleased at the elimination of an obstacle to her goal. The crown she never received is closer within reach.

C H A P T E R

2

❧

Gamble with Pride

The day after, Aminata meets an old friend of hers from before her father was elected to the office of grand councilor. Asani Juma, who is returning to the Ark Strikers' base in Diamondata from a mission near the border, is happy to finally meet her again after so long. He got his powers after encountering a man carrying krydium on the underground rapid transit line dropped some of it a year prior. The police confronted the criminal stealing these minerals to sell, prompting him to retaliate with the reptilian powers he gained. A piece of the material no larger than the palm of his hand got stuck in Asani's backpack before he ran away.

While he did not give it too much thought, he kept the small mineral with him. Three weeks passed until his power over magnetism came in. He could magnetize almost any alloy within his reach as well as produce magnetism in a focused space. Aminata cannot help but be impressed with how he has developed since the last time she saw him. He tells them he is about to "get even" with Ace.

Aminata is curious to know why he would have a quarrel with Ace. Asani clarifies that he is talking about gambling. The reason Maxim is called Ace is not just because of how good of a soldier he is but how good he is at gambling. Asani has lost to him twice, both with cards and competitive combat. Darion overhears and decides to join in.

9

At the barracks, Ace is on a winning streak with up to 2,000 Rimars won when Aminata, Takara, Tlalli, Darion, and Asani arrive. Ace smugly remarks Asani's attempt to beat him again. Asani makes a safe bet of 25 Rimars while Ace bets 525. A tense minute follows before a move is made. Asani fortunately wins with 400 in his hand. Though he can walk away as the victor, he decides that he wants to take all of Ace's winnings.

This unfortunately costs him all his winnings and leaves him with just 5 Rimars. With Asani defeated for a third time, Darion tries his luck at the table. He bet 250 while Ace bets 770. A tense game ensues for the next ten minutes before Darion wins with 1,020 Rimars in his hand. It is a rare loss for Ace, but he welcomes it. Darion hands 225 to Asani to commend him for his effort.

After the game, the soldiers venture to the department store in the city. Darion, Amadou, and Asani discuss what they want out of their careers. Asani wants to be a rich man with a big house and a beautiful wife. Amadou says, "Take it from me, a big house is not all that good." Darion questions what he would need with all that room.

Asani believes, with all the failures he has endured from being defeated by Ace to being defeated in competitive combat with other soldiers, a life of luxury is what he needs. Darion and Amadou remind him that they come from simple backgrounds with all their needs answered just as he has, so a life of luxury is just meaningless excess to them. Amadou questions if his third loss to Ace is getting to him when they are suddenly interrupted by a familiar man. Having overheard the son of the secretary of the Security Council, this lavender-suited man states that Ace cheated him out of 5,000 Rimars. Finding this odd since Ace is not fond of cheating, Amadou defends his comrade's honor.

Recognizing the son of the grand councilor, this man then tells them that he will collect his debt from the Vetrov family very soon. After he angrily storms off, Amadou recognizes him to be his father's rival, Morvolio Moretti. A prominent member of Parliament, Moretti has established a reputation for being a proud man with no intention for compromise. Ace is not thrown off or intimidated by the promise of antagonism not only because of who his father is but that he could not care less for what a man with a superiority complex thinks of him.

Aminata begins to take an interest in Darion and wants this time of rest to be an opportunity to get to know him better. She notices him conversing with a worker about a new jacket he has wanted for a while. Aminata has a slight hint of jealousy when she tells him she saw the jacket he wants on the next floor. The worker proceeds to present said jacket to him, much to Aminata's annoyance. As this worker notices the customer's displeasure, she tells her that she means no malice.

When the group decides to exit the massive store, Ace encounters two men approaching. He asks them if there is anything a soldier could help them with, to which they respond by attacking him. As the two krydian muggers try to rob him, he dodges their attack. The difference between the power of two untrained thugs and the skill of a well-trained krydian soldier is evident when Ace defeats them within seconds. Having knocked them unconscious, he assumes they were sent by Morvolio. Ace requests his comrades to accompany him to confront his adversary.

Aminata noticed him heading to the elevated train platform nearby. Unfortunately, the train takes off before the group can catch up to the politician. Takara suggests letting the commanding officers know, but Ace has other plans in mind. He follows Moretti's train to Champion Station, using his powers over the lights to conceal himself from any cameras or bystanders. Once Moretti leaves the train, he enters Rosellon National Bank.

Moretti carelessly knocks over the custodian's assistant bot in a fit of intense anger. The soldiers eavesdrop on his conversation with an assistant to hear him profess his disdain for what he deems to be "irritating cretins." He promises that the first thing he will do when he becomes grand councilor will be to fire General Vetrov and exile him. He then intends to assemble a greater legion of krydians to enforce whatever rules he sets out for Rosellon. Thinking he can bend Akamot to his will, he is adamant about gaining greater control of krydium even if it causes an all-out war.

The assistant questions if he realizes why that failed five years ago. Moretti responds by arrogantly stating that his strategy would have worked had he been prime minister at the time of the failed incursion. Ace is eager to teach Moretti a lesson for the assault, but Takara and Aminata remind him that they will be reprimanded for using their powers against a member of parliament. It is then that the reason for Moretti's visit comes out when he discreetly takes a data pack with him. Against the advice of his fellow soldiers, Ace follows Morvolio to the train.

Grabbing the back of his collar, Ace says, "Sending goons to take your money back wasn't smart now, was it?" Confused at this soldier's aggressive nature, Morvolio warns him not to pick a fight with a member of parliament. Ace wonders if it is because he might be weak, but his enemy reveals to him that he is a krydian with power over emotion. The ever-confident soldier doubts the effectiveness of this ability.

To his bewilderment, the politician responds with an emotion-charged attack that bends a nearby support beam. Enraged, Morvolio tells him that he does not care who his father is because no man shall accost him. A fight across the rail lines ensues. The two exchange strikes and dodge oncoming trains until they reach Parliament Station.

Morvolio is left tired out by the exchange and subdued by his adversary. Capitol guards arrive to assess the situation; among them is Ace's older brother, Vissarion Vetrov. After Ace relays his reasons that led to him fighting the leader of the opposition, Morvolio is detained on suspicion. When the men who accosted the general's younger son regain consciousness, they tell the interrogators that Moretti called them with a promise of reward for robbing Maxim Vetrov. Since the call was made using an open line, a recording of the call matches Morvolio's voice down to his laugh.

Now disgraced for his actions, Morvolio Moretti is disqualified from the election for grand councilor. Although it is not what he wanted, His Eminence is now left with no viable challenger to his position. Maxim is called to his commander's office to answer why he was in a quarrel with the leader of the opposition. He tells Lieutenant

Yamashita that he was taking a walk out with his comrades when those men attacked him. Since good reasoning has been given, he avoids reprimand. The lieutenant still criticizes her subordinate for provoking a quarrel with a very high-profile politician but is happy to see that he held his own against his foes.

In gratitude for his loyalty, Aminata and the others tell the lieutenant that Moretti attacked him unprovoked. Although the young Vetrov did nothing wrong in defending himself, toying with the emotions of one who is so proud and arrogant can be dangerous. After he leaves to tend to other tasks, the lieutenant smiles and lets out a small laugh all too much like Morvolio's.

After they return to the base, Aminata comes across Captain Ichimada as she is walking with Takara and Tlalli. While her two fellow soldiers walk on, she stays to talk with the captain about her recent experiences. In a dulcet tone, Captain Ichimada says, "I hope you've liked being a soldier so far."

Aminata responds, "Going after a rogue army feels riveting, madam." The captain then asks her subordinate the most important question. Their dialogue is as follows:

> Rika: Do you feel proud?
> Aminata: A little uneasy.
> Rika: About what?
> Aminata: Vaughn. I get that he was the enemy,
>   but I have never ended someone's existence.
> Rika: You have nothing to be ashamed of. Vaughn
>   was nothing more than a fat drunken pawn
>   who thought he could be king.
> Aminata: Have you ever killed anyone?
> Rika: Yes, of course.
> Aminata: What was it like?
> Rika: A fast rush of emotions crashing like a wave.
>   To spill blood is to surrender your innocence.
> Aminata: Is that what I did by killing Vaughn?

Rika: No, he may be dead because of your actions,
     but you still hold on to your mercy. The first
     person I killed was very close to me.
Aminata: Sounds like my sense of loyalty is being
     tested.
Rika: Because it is. It is to be learned with strug-
     gle, and you will come to that soon.
Aminata: Thanks, madam.
Rika: Please, call me Rika when your comrades are
     not around. You and I are equals, Aminata.

The young corporal admires the captain for her generosity and places her full faith and trust with her. Captain Ichimada has a concrete assurance to liquidate all those who dare to make themselves renegades. Those who have been captured for working with the rogue mayor are set for execution. She is enthusiastic to see Corporal Keita further improve her skill with her abilities and to continue to be wise. The young corporal accepts that the loss of life is a part of the service she chose to take on as she prepares for her next mission.

3

Sink into the Dark

THE MINISTRY OF INTELLIGENCE HAS CAUGHT WIND of a Phantom Sword network operating in the south of the capital, planning an attack on the National Media headquarters. Ark Strikers Unit 380 is ordered to root them out. Among them is a notorious traitor with mastery over ice named Dolion Acquafredda also known as Cold Kill. He has stolen five million Rimars in property and killed thirteen State Police officers and five civilians in his tenure as a krydian renegade. More crudely, he tends to taunt the authorities just after his attacks.

Lieutenant Yamashita assigns Aminata, Takara, and Xochitl to this mission to assist the targets and capture the individuals responsible. The State Police have requested krydian assistance with a supply delivery at one in the afternoon. As the renegade forces of Phantom Sword are likely to attack the delivery, conventional means will not suffice. Meeting the delivery workers just outside of Diamondata, one is taken aback by Xochitl's cold demeanor before apologizing. He then says he is thankful that she is helping them. Sitting inside, the soldiers pass the time with a game of spades.

Aminata decides to take the time to get to know her fellow troops better. Speaking to Takara, she asks her about her life before she became a krydian. She had a fun life in Violet View with her aunt and uncle. They taught her to be humble with others. Upon receiving her powers during the incident at her job, she fled the city and sought refuge in the capital of Diamondata. She found another job but failed to connect with her fellow workers due to their disinterest in her.

It was on the fifth of November in 2179 when she was sitting on a bench enjoying ice cream in Dorothy Park, then she was approached by a woman in uniform. Lieutenant Yamashita offered her a chance to hone her skill with her abilities and to put a stop to the group that drove her away from the city she loved. She has since reconnected with her mother and sisters, but since they are so busy, she cannot spend time with them like she wants.

Xochitl remarks her time before she became a krydian as joyfully dreary and occasionally remarkable. She has always found a gray overcast or the night to be more beautiful than a bright sunny day. When the kids did not let her play or hang out with them, her father would cheer her up with a song. Her mother would make her the best salads and only got her a cake at celebrations like her birthday or graduation. Tlalli kept her from getting into fights but never saw any reason to let her win in any manner of competition.

The truck is sent careening by a sheet of black ice. After crashing, the soldiers try to escape to the back of the truck, only to realize the door is frozen over. Takara is dazed by the crash while Aminata touches the door to focus the cold energy to convert it to a heat energy strike to break the door open. The trio gets out to see Dolion and several of his operatives leaving with supplies. Just before they can chase after him, he laughs as he kills a downed guard and detonates an ice bomb to shroud his escape.

After he disappears, Aminata looks around to see five dead guards. Takara tends to the sole surviving guard while Xochitl walks over to see the downed guard with an ice spear in his chest. Aminata walks over to her comrade, asking how she is feeling. Xochitl fails to immediately respond, having to process the harrowing sight before her. The chaos, the icy mist, and the long sharp piece of ice left in a man's chest is exactly how she found her dead father in the street.

Now knowing exactly who her father's killer is, she asks for her sister to come along in the mission to find where Phantom Sword is operating in the city. The waterfall of tears they shed are still fresh in their memory. On Takara's advice, Lieutenant Yamashita endorses the Valiente sisters' intention to hunt down Dolion. Since this will have to take place at night, Xochitl will have an edge. She thinks to herself about the moment her powers came forth.

It was a dark rainy day just a week after the funeral. She was lying down in her bed listening to dark classical music, not wanting to be bothered. She kept her eyes closed as the song immersed her in sorrow. She opened her eyes once she noticed the song fading. Her whole room was covered in Vantablack.

She was standing in her room confused, and her sister then came home talking about the steel beam she bent. Tlalli accidentally broke her sister's door when she ran into her room. She was calming down, and the room's deep-dark color dissipated to reveal the krydium glow on the jacket Xochitl borrowed from Tlalli. Understanding they were now gifted with extraordinary abilities, they joined the Army of Rosellon to put an end to the man who ruined their lives and the army he belonged to.

While incognito, Dolion stops by the neighborhood market. He unreasonably requests the entire box of apples for 2 Rimars. After the shopkeeper rejects this demand, Dolion destroys the table and threatens the man in front of his family. Scared for his life, the shopkeeper backs away to allow this brute to steal a box of his best fruit. Fortunately, a bystander reports the incident to the State Police. They then relay the information to the army, who pinpoint the location of the renegade network.

Asani helps Tlalli get ready for the raid on renegade operations. Tlalli remarks on how she would try to sing the songs for her sister but did not have the voice for it. She took to making her sister's favorite salads since their mother had to recover from the emotional wreck. He asks, "Was this the reason you decided to become a soldier?"

She says, "Yes, we can't let another family endure our pain."

At eleven in the night, Unit 380 is sent to terminate Phantom Sword's network in Diamondata. At his base, Dolion expresses his gleeful excitement at another successful task carried out. A message from Prince Toshiki warns him not to strain the resources he has been provided with on a personal matter. The weapons he stole are meant to target the capitol complex and not to be wasted. Dolion says, "I need to have fun when I follow orders."

Dolion is feeling extra cocky until he notices the unnatural silence. As his section of the renegade forces have been hiding out in the living spaces on Lucielle Avenue, he expected more noise from the youth on summer break from school around him. The quiet is terminated by a loud bang that destroys the wall in front of him. The capital sector of the State Police begins their raid. Dolion starts running downstairs to be greeted by more heavily armed officers.

He deploys a wall of ice to cover his escape into the tunnel nearby. One of his fellow renegades uses the mech stored away in the garage to fight the authorities. Tlalli channels the severely damaging power through her poleax to incapacitate the machine. Aminata drains the lights of their electric energy to cause the renegades to run into Dorothy Park.

The three remaining hostiles are separated, running into the thick trees. The first thinks he has a clear path to escape, but he sees a fast-moving quiet figure behind him. Although the figure steps on every twig and disturbs every bird and squirrel, not a single sound is heard. Heart beating out of his chest, he runs faster. He spots a fast electric bike, thinking to use it to get away, but his silent doom has caught up.

Lieutenant Zynda Yamashita ceases his run with a silenced slash to his legs. Bleeding profusely, the disabled traitor tries to yell for help, with no sound to come from his mouth. All he can hear is the giggle from the lieutenant savoring her kill. She then gleefully says, "Thank you for making this so much fun. He was too slow." Zynda shows the bloodied glove that belonged to his confederate who also attempted to escape through the park before viciously cutting him down.

Now alone, Dolion takes a second to catch his breath. The light next to him starts flickering before abruptly going out. One by one, every light near him loses its energy and goes out. He is helplessly stuck in the dark next to a pond. Knowing the pond leads to safety, he freezes it to start running again.

The ice is then cracked by a strike from a furious Tlalli. The crack opens to cause him to trip and twist his ankle. With nowhere left to run, he realizes he is surrounded. Crawling over to the ground, he looks up to see Xochitl with her scythe in hand. He tries to fend off the soldier with an ice spear that is quickly shattered.

Dolion pleads for mercy, then tries one last time to attack by knocking over a light post. Tlalli knocks it away to come towering over the man who killed her father. Xochitl tells him, "Any kindness is wasted on you." She bends the pitch-black surrounding her to wrap around her scythe. Finally, she brings down the blade into her enemy's chest to consume him in shadow.

With nothing left of him, the Valiente sisters hug to the joy of having avenged their beloved father. They thank their comrades for their help. At the base, the captain asks how her soldiers feel after their mission. Xochitl then states, "I feel alive," and wears the widest smile she has ever struck. Her mother has arrived to visit with great news. She has learned how to sing the song to warm her daughters' hearts.

4

Malice and Consequence

In Violet View, Prince Toshiki Ichimada berates his subordinates for their failure to assassinate the grand councilor. Since they were responsible for organizing the failed attempt on His Eminence, he demands an explanation as to why they did not use a more effective method with krydians or explosives. They explain that they were not able to get either of those past the tight security at his daughter's graduation and thus had to use the guns left for them before. An incoming covert message from his niece recommends that the prince should assign a task to the most frightening krydian in his ranks. Prince Toshiki winces at this advice since he knows whom this is referring to.

Lieutenant Yamashita briefs the soldiers on a manufacturing company suspected of providing arms directly to the renegades. Icon Tech is known for manufacturing high-quality weapons used by the Army of Rosellon. Some weapons they produced were also found in the possession of the Phantom Sword assassins that attacked the grand councilor. The soldiers are told about a potential whistleblower of theirs working with someone in the company. Darion along with Takara, Ace, Tlalli, and Xochitl are sent to a branch of Icon Tech's operations in the west part of the city to search for their potential whistleblower.

The company's high executive, Tyson Catcher, insists he has been doing his best to stop the flow of his company's supplies to

Phantom Sword. This has done little to deter suspicions. Just as the group begins to settle, they notice a man walk out of the building. He is noticeably on edge and trying not to be seen walking out with a letter he places into his jacket pocket. The man is Icon Tech's chief of research and development, Dr. Isai Valeka Orozco. Xochitl distracts him while he conspicuously insists that everything is fine and takes the item. They find out Dr. Orozco's younger of two sons, Orson, has been kidnapped by Phantom Sword.

He was on his way to reason with the renegades when he found out who exactly kidnapped him. The soldiers are all stunned when they see the perpetrator's given name is Malicine. She has attained a reputation as a notorious Phantom Sword operative known for playing malicious games with her targets. The penalty for failing these games will be either humiliation, fear, pain, or death. She is a sadistic woman, and her identity is yet to be known.

For the past two weeks, she has abducted four men who occupy positions as leaders or officials to relatives of them. While the authorities have had a challenging time pinpointing her location, abilities, or her motives, but she benefits greatly from being a renegade soldier. The letter is a frightening poem that reads,

> I offered you kindness, but you chose cruel
>   blindness.
> The heaven you seek is up above with my pure
>   love.
> You have wronged me in the worst way; now it is
>   time to pay.
> Your decadence that knows no bounds will send
>   them into the ground.
> The stage will be set at my behest, so do not rest.
> The folly of your avarice will be answered with
>   my malice!

Dr. Orozco is eager for the safe return of his son, but Catcher is hesitant. He believes negotiating with her would yield no success and declines any notion of ransom. While Malicine has sought ransom, she is motivated to get what she perceives to be the truth from those she antagonizes. With her stage almost set, they are frightened at what she has in store. Since they know nothing about her, they have no idea what to do.

After relaying the news to the rest, Aminata becomes anxious. Captain Ichimada wants them to be ready to find Malicine when she triggers her plan. Since the cruel renegade gave no warning as to when exactly that would be, they must be patient. Ace feels impatient since she has abducted four and might likely take many more. Xochitl says it could just be one or a few since the malicious poem said, "The stage is almost set." All the answers to their questions are answered when a message is broadcast directly to them.

There on the screens, in all her sinister glory, is Malicine. Donning an eerily frightening mask concealing her face, she happily states, "The stage is complete," before revealing her final abductee. The atmosphere inside the base is rife with intensity but none more so than Aminata. The fifth man captured is revealed to be her brother, Amadou.

She asks, "My brother? What has he done to deserve this?" with fury. Takara asks her if Amadou knew anyone who might hold a grudge. The captain allows her to embark on her brother's rescue with close supervision. Should they or the unwilling contestants of her game not comply with her rules, they will face severe penalty.

The first captive contestant is a young man who serves in Diamondata's city council named Layton Lochlan. He has two chances to answer the question honestly or face the consequences. With fear all over his body, Malicine asks him, "What makes you abandon your principles?"

He shakenly replies, "Is it money?" Unfortunately for him, money is close to the answer but not what she wants. Shaking, he then answers, "Power."

Again, unfortunately, the answer is wrong. The penalty is humiliation. Going from scared to confused, he then becomes smug at what seems like a light consequence. Malicine then tells him, "If your life ever had value, you wouldn't feel the need to be above everyone."

This insult that anyone would seem to shrug off easily shatters Layton's very essence to a thousand pieces. He desperately exclaims "No, NO, NO!" as any semblance of his former self disappears. Falling to the ground in total shame, he is sane no more.

Malicine then gleefully states that the answer is love and hate. The dual answer confuses every onlooker as to its fairness. Aminata and her comrades do not have long to locate where the captives are kept. Each question she asks them slowly reveals who she is and her connection to them. She believes she might have known who Malicine used to be.

The next man is Phillip Phobos VI, son of the commissioner of Rosellon National Bank. The penalty for his failure will be fear. Quaking in his pristine shoes, he wonders what more she can do to him with that punishment. She asks him, "Do you ever feel remorse?"

He replies, "For what?"

She says, "For your betrayal, carelessness, and greed." Takara thinks the question is so vague and unfair that it seems like she wants him to give the wrong answer.

The captain says the purpose of this twisted game is to punish them for what wrong she believes they have done. To elaborate, Malicine says that Phillip knew a lady before the meteorite struck and abandoned her for another lady with what he thought were beautiful abilities with flowers. When that lady he left gained abilities of her own, she tried to impress him to get him back. To her dismay, he married his new beautiful flower girl. Philip calmly says, "It was five years ago, a lot has happened, and I can't remember every time some girl gave her heart to me."

Philip looks up to see pure fury in Malicine's eyes through her mask. What stares back into his eyes is nothing less than pure terror. This stops his speech and causes him to bellow out in the worst fear he has ever felt in his life. Not one ounce of bravery remains as he cries a river of tears for mercy. The Ark Strikers believe this enemy's ability could be causation manipulation or emotional control.

Judging by Malicine's methods and targeting, Aminata deduces her ability to be consequence control. The consequence of any wrong that has been done to her is being inflicted on her abductees with no mercy. It might sound absurd, but krydium seems to also affect how a person interacts with their environment mentally. The good news is that they now have an area where they might be. Time is winding down before she gets to the last contestant.

The captive facing the penalty of pain is Orson Orozco. Malicine tells him about a time he failed to help a lady in need. When she needed help after twisting her ankle on the subway, he walked by with indifference instead of helping her. She asks him why he would be so careless. His response only enrages her more when he states, "It just didn't seem like something I should do, so I just let someone else worry about it." Right away, he suffers the penalty.

Every single spot where Orson can feel pain is targeted. He falls to the ground riving in agony until he passes out from the pain in the longest five seconds of his life. Believing this is his fault, Dr. Orozco cannot stand to watch his beloved son suffer. He starts blaming Catcher for not negotiating for his son's release. Luckily, the Ark Strikers are close to the target location in Phantom Sword territory.

The man designated for the punishment of death is the vice minister of defense, Edmund Walker. Before Malicine can ask the question, he foolishly interrupts. He shouts, "I do my job well, and there's nothing you can say that will make me regret anything!"

His captor says, "Do people not die because of your job?"

The vice minister states, "Does it matter if we have some collateral damage every now and then? Some responsibilities require a little death."

Continuing his callous tirade, he stops midsentence to collapse to the ground. The vice minister is dead, and Malicine proceeds to the last man. She asks him what the opposite of callousness and cruelty is. Wisely, Amadou responds, "Compassion."

She asks him, "What lesson have you learned?"

With no fear on his face, the grand councilor's son replies, "Indifference and callousness must always come at a price."

His devious abductor is pleased with his answer. Confident that he is different from the others, she allows him to question what her motivation is. She asserts that malice and consequence must always accompany each other. As someone who occupies a high place in society, Malicine believes she had to save Amadou from falling into decadence. By punishing individuals in the higher social strata, she frightens anyone who would be indifferent to the misfortune of someone who is kind. When he asks who she is, she touches his chin, looks directly into his eyes, and replies, "I am here to save you."

Just in time to put an end to this twisted game are Aminata and Takara storming into the room. Stopping before they risk failure, Aminata approaches Malicine. While Takara rescues the unwilling contestants starting with Amadou, Corporal Keita grabs a chair and converses with the renegade to avoid the effect of her ability. Their dialogue is as follows:

> Aminata: You frighten millions for what? Justice.
> Malicine: Yes. Everyone needs to see the example of the justice they need.
> Aminata: And even if it's cruel, you think you have to make a point at the cost of people's sanity?
> Malicine: They must know that there will be a consequence for any wrong they have done.
> Aminata: You're forgetting something important.
> Malicine: Oh, really now?
> Aminata: You are traumatizing innocent people, and that means you must face a consequence.
> Malicine: No, because as I just said, the consequence I show them prevents them from falling into decadence.
> Aminata: You think they function like these men you abducted.
> Malicine: There is always a chance.
> Aminata: That is the problem: chance. It means they also have an opportunity to not do the same acts, and you are corrupting the outcome.
> Malicine: You make a good point, but that does not mean I should stop.

Aminata's slowly charged blast explodes on the floor. As she anticipated this, this allows Malicine to escape with the help of her fellow renegades. Takara reminds her that they need to seek immediate medical attention for the captives. With her identity unknown, Malicine will continue to pose a mystery as much as a threat.

The public backlash is riveting at the terror wrought in front of them. Not simply a deranged psychopath, Malicine proved a point while shattering their collective sense of security. Her ability to compromise those who were well guarded not only puzzles the authorities but has shown that anyone is vulnerable. The survivors are treated for their trauma with Amadou being all but fine while the rest will need more time to recover. Though the vice minister of defense was assassinated, the man to suffer the most is High Executive Tyson Catcher.

Icon Tech supplies are revealed to have been in Malicine's possession. Catcher is arrested by the military police while still denying all charges of aiding the renegade paramilitary. Dr. Orozco ascends to the company's top position of high executive as a result of the military's takeover of the company. With the military in control of the company, Dr. Orozco assures his loyalty without question.

Though Captain Ichimada is slightly disappointed by the failure of her soldiers to capture such a significant threat, there is an opportunity before her. Dr. Orozco trusts her for being responsible for his son's rescue. She acknowledges her uncle for placing a competent combatant in his employ just as she has in hers. Malicine will continue her reign of fear as the captain's plans inch closer to fruition.

5

His Power Is Destruction!

FOLLOWING HER DARING RESCUE OF HER BROTHER, Aminata decides to train more efficiently by taking part in competitive combat. With the permission of her superior officers, she takes it upon herself to choose her opponents. She has piqued interest in sparring against Xochitl, but her sister has been looking forward to matching their powers for a while and volunteers. Power over energy meets power over damage with no krydian weapons to pose the risk of serious harm. The two have five minutes to complete their session.

Tlalli allows Aminata to deliver the first strike. Slightly thrown off by this generosity in combat, she grants the request with a swift energized kick. To her surprise, the damage dealt by the kick not only failed to harm Tlalli but empowered her. She responds with a punch to send Aminata into the air. After stopping herself from flying across the base, Corporal Keita feels what should have been a minor hit due to her defense cling to her arm she used to block the strike.

The damage creates a slight bruise that motivates her to ease back down to the surface and send an energy attack through the ground. Tlalli uses it to propel herself toward her opponent with an intense smash to the ground below. Dodging again, Corporal Keita attempts a buzz saw kick that is caught by Corporal Valiente's strong hand. It seems to everyone that the fight is won when Tlalli disables Aminata with a mid-damage punch to her gut. She stands high and mighty with victory and says, "You fought well, but the more experienced combatant always has the advantage." Just when she offers a hand to help her up, Aminata drains Tlalli's physical energy to render her too tired to fight any longer with just ten seconds left on the clock.

Victorious, Aminata states, "Then you should know a better strategy is always key." Tlalli rises from the ground in defeat to allow her comrade to reenergize her. She praises her ability to think so well in combat. Aminata jokingly says, "It felt like you were trying to knock me all the way to Akamot with that punch." Before Takara starts her sparring session with Asani, she notes to Darion that even though her two friends are cordial with each other, they have now become rivals. As this has been productive training, it will serve the soldiers well in their mission at the grand councilor's request.

Grand Councilor Adama Keita has received an urgent warning from the chairman of the State Council of Akamot, Tokala Hatahali. It regards a krydian with a powerful ability coming to Rosellon. Suspecting him to be in the employ of Prince Toshiki Ichimada, the army interrogates the renegades in their captivity on any information they can find on him. The only thing they can tell the authorities about him is what they have heard. With methods he believes to be merciful, he is unrelenting in his one-man crusade against the concept of order. Hysterical at the military's growing power in Rosellon, he has set out on a personal mission to save the people from tyranny.

His Eminence issues a warning for the citizens on his actions. He issues an organized search order to the State Police, the civil guard, and the army. Civilian authorities have failed to counter his abilities with their standard countermeasures for krydian enemies. This prompts the action of krydian soldiers to neutralize him. Because what he can do with his krydian ability has been so puzzling, his power has simply been called destruction.

Aminata, Darion, Takara, Ace, and Tlalli head to the site of his last attack in the east side of the capital to find out where he might be next. Upon finding what had been the office of Colonel Felton to be destroyed, they ask witnesses to describe the attacker. They say he had brown skin, wavy black hair, a goatee, and stood at around 180 centimeters. He wore a dark-green shirt with black pants, mahogany-brown boots, and a gray coat. With an axe to grind and immense power at his disposal, he is known to the public as Dahak.

Aminata takes a second to rest while pondering what she thought being a soldier would entail. Having just dealt with the deranged cunning of Malicine three weeks prior, she did not expect to face a threat with such immense power so soon. A man next to her notices her frustration. He says, "I can tell you're not having a good time in that uniform right about now." Their conversation is as follows:

> Aminata: I just faced a psychopath who abducted my brother, tortured three high-profile men, and assassinated a high-ranking official.
>
> The man: I watched the whole thing. She was quite frightening.
>
> Aminata: Like I had enough trouble with trying to stop Toshiki, now I have a major receipt for one of his soldiers.
>
> The man: That weight comes with the uniform. Things like that are bound to happen when you throw a lot of weight on your shoulders.
>
> Aminata: I would be lying if I said I wasn't having second thoughts. Having these powers doesn't change it.
>
> The man: That is the principal nature of being a protector. You are the one who faces the toughest challenges so others will not.

Aminata reminds herself of what the captain said and accepts the wise words of the man who gives his name as Bikram Patil. After Mr. Patil leaves, Darion relays some latest information they just received about Dahak. He was once a soldier for Rosellon who fought in the war for krydium five years ago. As the sole survivor of his unit of fifteen, he was taken by Akamot as a prisoner of war when his power emerged in his cell. This man has the potential to be the country's biggest internal stand-alone threat, and Aminata seeks answers from him.

Meanwhile, Mr. Patil is checking into his room when he notices a young boy looking for his parents. Without a slight hint of hesitation, he takes some time away from trying to relax so that he can help the boy reunite with his parents. The boy's mother rewards him with extra money to stay at the hotel. Upon reaching his room, he gathers his intel for his plan to assassinate Major General Ryoko Ichimada.

Bikram Patil, whose long pacifism was ended by the concerning increase of the military's power, has taken on the identity of Dahak to exact his justice upon those responsible for the deaths of his comrades. He can still recall seeing fourteen bodies lying out as if the event happened just ten minutes ago. As the king has not been seen for the past five years, his ire is directed at Major General Ryoko Ichimada. She was personally responsible for his fate on the front line even more so than her husband or her brother-in-law.

Queen Ryoko believed he and his fourteen comrades would be the most adept at protecting her when she decided to head to the front lines. Prior to the strike, he ate with the general alongside his comrades. A soldier said he wanted to see what material they were fighting over, to which the queen responded by taking out a piece of krydium from her jacket. The queen said, "This is far too precious for the enemy to have." Stepping out to get some fresh air, she saw an incoming projectile the rest of the soldiers inside her camp could not hear with their partying. She ran without giving notice to the soldiers inside.

Her reasoning was that she did not have enough time to warn anyone else. Five Royal Guards were all that remained after Dahak's unit was annihilated. With a callous demeanor, she showed no emotion for the carnage around her and left with a piece of krydium as Dahak was taken as a prisoner of war when he regained consciousness.

In a week, Major General Ichimada will lead an operation against Phantom Sword to the town of Autumn Green. That will be the day Dahak exacts his vengeance upon his enemy that represents the folly of order, and he will not allow anyone to stand in his way. In two days, he will be checking out of the hotel to travel to the town.

Unbeknownst to him, Ryoko Ichimada's daughters will be close to her. Adding to Dahak's challenge will be a few other skilled krydian soldiers accompanying them. While he is only one man against the army, he will ardently take that risk to put a stop to the growing tyranny and to avenge his slain comrades.

6

Fall into Eternal Peace

Darion and Asani discuss how Amadou will approach his feel-ings for Takara. Darion suggests that he just be as natural as he can when approaching her while Asani insists on a display of extravagance to entice her. Amadou has a tough time deciding what to do when Xochitl emerges from his shadow. She overheard what they were talking about and tells them going over the top is too risky. "You may as well beat yourself over the head right now because using all your energy to impress her is just going to drive her away."

Xochitl explains that if he wants everything to go well with Takara, he must be patient for the right moment. Darion says, "You're assigned to patrol the Gordon District in the south of the capital along with us. Takara will be with us too." Before they head to Autumn Green, he should get to know her better. As a last bit of advice, Xochitl tells him that Takara has feelings for him, and he should let her know what kind of relationship he wants.

In the Gordon District, the two begin to connect. Amadou notices something bothering her. Their conversation is as follows:

> Amadou: You all right?
> Takara: Yeah, it's my family.
> Amadou: Are they okay?
> Takara: They put me under a lot of pressure.
> Amadou: Are they respecting you?

Takara: Yes, you ever feel like love can also be wrong?
Amadou: I think I can picture that. Does it make
    you regret being a soldier?
Takara: No, but it does give *me another struggle.*

Amadou cannot converse with her any longer as he believes it is not yet the time. His fear of failure continues to weigh heavily on his shoulders. The pair then proceed to their new positions at Lieutenant Yamashita's request. Fatouma is disappointed with her brother for failing to confess his feelings. He is reminded that the chance could disappear at any moment.

Meanwhile, Dahak travels through the countryside in preparation for his vengeance. Unable to take the train, he rides a bike to the site of the upcoming battle. Wearing his old uniform for the first time in five years, he is aware that his path to vengeance will end in his demise. If he is to die, then he shall do so wearing a symbol of his self-sacrifice. While feeling the wind blow through his hair, he calls back to the time before he chose to wear it for the first time.

It was a cold snowy winter in February of 2164 when he was a twenty-year-old man unable to find a job willing to accept him. The opportunity of a steady career path promised by the Royal Army of Rosellon motivated him to join. Out of this, he made a family with a nurse he met in his service. His daughter turned thirteen two weeks prior to his deployment to the front line in the king's incursion. Arriving, he waits just outside of the town for the arrival of the army to confront Phantom Sword.

Several military vehicles accompanied by powerful krydian soldiers come into view while Dahak patiently awaits the battle to commence. Meanwhile, his enemy is speaking with her daughter on the matter of what is to come. The major general asks her daughter if she finds anything useful in this scorned soldier. Captain Ichimada tells her mother, "Even if he were not hell-bent on assassinating you, I would still have no use for him or his senseless ability. He is a broken mess." Major General Ichimada is pleased to know her daughters have all done well to remain hidden in plain sight.

Trusting her firstborn daughter to guard her, she asks her what she would be doing if she did not have her crown on her mind, to which Rika responds, "I guess I would be living some mediocre happy life with a husband and a family of my own."

Ryoko replies, "I would love that for you, but I know your ambitions are too great for mediocrity." Captain Ichimada orders Aminata and Darion to the edge of the town before the first strikes are delivered. Ark Strikers and regular soldiers discreetly get into position. On the major general's command, they begin their battle to liberate the town.

Amadou and Takara remain with the major general while she advances. Just as the army has brought their best soldiers, Phantom Sword has brought their best renegades. The captain crushes a battalion of enemies with pressure strikes and repels their shots with her repulsion field. The chaotic scene is turning to the army's benefit until suddenly a wave of pure destruction eliminates soldiers on both sides. Aminata looks in the direction of the wave to see a familiar face.

The man who introduced himself to her as Bikram Patil has begun his attack. Confused, Aminata quickly realizes that this man in uniform showing no regard for the others wearing the same attire is the enemy she was searching for. Dahak approaches the major general's location with fury. In the confusion, Takara stays at the major general's side to guard her against the threat of this lone enemy.

Amadou rushes to her side, not wanting her to be harmed. As she swore to protect her brother at all costs, Aminata makes up her mind to send a concentrated energy strike in Dahak's direction. Bewildered, he says, "Can you not see the injustice you serve?"

Aminata responds, "I'm protecting my family." While Dahak sympathizes with her, he will not allow his opportunity for retribution to go to waste.

In their fierce battle, the young corporal negates the destructive energy thrown by the old warrant officer. He warns her the woman behind her is her true enemy. Knowing he is not of complete ill will, Aminata tries to restrict herself from killing him. Captain Ichimada assists her subordinate by bringing down a column snapped from a nearby building. Stunned, Dahak attempts to send another wave when Aminata cuts the back of his knees to incapacitate him.

Believing that he is defeated, Aminata tells him he will be taken in as a prisoner of war. It is then that Dahak gets ready to send yet another path of destruction toward Major General Ichimada. Amadou is left stuck under some heavy debris just behind the general and cannot move. Disregarding any self-preservation instincts, Takara refuses to leave his side. Aminata has no choice but to cut Dahak's arms with a cross-sickle slash just one split second before the captain can intervene. With no way to send out any attacks, he is defeated.

Suddenly, a shot rings out. Aminata looks over to see a smoking gun in the general's hand and a hole in Dahak's heart. He warns Aminata not to allow herself to become a tool for treachery as his unrelenting fury subsides to an eternal peace. With a tear in her eye, the general hugs Takara and commends Aminata for her bravery. The man known as Dahak is dead, and the army carries on with its victory against the renegades.

After her daunting experience, Aminata speaks with her mother and sister in the palace garden. Fadimata blooms her daughter's favorite lily and tells her that as long as she and Adama were around, no child of theirs was going to be a tool. Fatouma says, "What matters is that you saved our brother."

At the base, Takara and Amadou cool their nerves from an intense battle. Following her display of bravery in Autumn Green, Takara asks how he is feeling. He felt like his fear of failure disappeared in that moment. She tells him that she was not going to stop trying to get that debris off him until he was safe. They gaze into each other's eyes and share a passionate kiss.

A Journey for Resolve

With the crisis further straining the civilian authorities in the capital, Major General Ryoko Ichimada holds an important meeting with the grand councilor. In the august company of His Eminence, she advises Grand Councilor Keita of the drastic measures he will need to take to restore peace to the country. His Eminence argues that the people would not welcome advanced militarization. She tells him that the citizens of Rosellon are so gripped by the fear of the crisis that they would be willing to sacrifice a few civil liberties to have peace. More concerningly, Ryoko notifies him of high-ranking officers perceiving him to be weak in the face of trepidation, especially General Vetrov. The grand councilor is left with no choice but to declare martial law and grant the army the right to maintain security in the capital.

Darion, who was present at High Executive Catcher's arrest, recalls a conversation he overheard between two workers. This pair remarked on how they would be so well rewarded for carrying out their jobs that they would be able to live in their own penthouses on the highest towers in the capital. Darion was perplexed by this ambition because their jobs pay them well to sustain a good living. With the convenient timing of this conversation and the arrest of their boss, Darion held suspicions of the nature of Catcher's arrest.

Before he could act on his suspicion of these two workers, he was called away by General Vetrov. The questions of who they are, where they went, and who else they could be working for remain open. Jack remarks that since the military now has control of Icon Tech, it is only a matter of time before those two suspicious workers and anyone assisting them are found. Three crates of vital supplies also went missing from that warehouse at that time.

Darion's suspicion remains even with his next mission ahead. The Ark Strikers are set to go on a mission toward the center of the renegades' operation. Under the control of the Army of the Phantom Sword, the town is acting as a base for the rogue paramilitary's operations. Their next destination is none other than Darion's hometown of Hollow Mine.

General Vetrov leads 20,000 soldiers in the operation to the town of Hollow Mine with Captain Ichimada and Lieutenant Yamashita's company of 180 powerful soldiers. Darion had to leave his home because of the renegade army taking control. Aminata can see how personal this is for Darion and does her best to comfort him since he will be in the town he was born in for the first time in five years. "You had my back in Swan Silver. I have your back here," Aminata says with full sincerity.

Darion feels comforted with having someone he can deeply trust at his side. Knowing that he is about to defend his home from the renegade army, the pressure hits a very personal note for him. When the Ark Strikers arrive, they are greeted by a flurry of hostility. Darion's chief concern is the safety of his cousin who chose to stay in the town to help his neighbors. An enemy grabs his cousin to hold him hostage.

Knowing there is no chance for victory, she threatens Darion's cousin with a gun to his head to secure an escape from the battlefield. Asani magnetizes the gun to take it away from the renegade before Amadou subdues her.

There is hope for an end to this crisis on the Ark Strikers' next immediate destination. Led by Captain Ichimada, they are determined to neutralize the leader of the Army of the Phantom Sword, Toshiki Ichimada. The former prime minister has remained in the city of Violet View. The army is poised to root out the nation's former head of government and take him back alive or otherwise. As the leader of the very organization that motivated her into combat, Aminata is willing to use any means to dispose of the former prime minister.

On the journey to her hometown, Takara remarks at how she has wanted to return to her home city for almost five years. Though she had her powers when Phantom Sword began their operations, she was nowhere near skilled enough to take on a rebel army by herself. She is excited to enjoy everything the beautiful city of Violet View has to offer with her friends and family once again. She looks forward to a special moment of peace.

Aminata asks her best friend, "Anyone you want to share that special moment with?"

Takara then states, "Funny you ask, since he's—" Before she can fully answer her best friend's question, she is interrupted by an abrupt quake in the ground. They have arrived.

Just after coming off their hard-fought victory in Hollow Mine the day before, they are just in time to greet a much tougher challenge. Serving as the prime base of operations for the renegade army, Violet View is far more dangerous than Swan Silver. On every block, there was an enemy. On every street, there was a weapon. In every building, there was a trap.

The defense assembled by Toshiki Ichimada makes Quincy Vaughn's defenses look like toy soldiers. Krydian renegades at the city center fiercely confront the army, killing twenty regulars and wounding Jack before he can get his defense up. It is Aminata, Darion, and Takara who manage to defeat four strong enemy soldiers. The last one, an enemy capable of incorporating metal into his body, fights Aminata. This makes him a perfect target for a magnetic energy blast to his legs followed by a double-sickle energy slash to his gut.

Tlalli and Xochitl encounter a squad of krydian enemies with heat abilities and regulars with weapons. The damage they inflict on Tlalli only empowers her to annihilate five of them. Xochitl kills the remaining four by using their shadows to consume them. Another krydian enemy attempts to hit them with an ice harpoon, only to be cut in half by Xochitl's scythe. Ace disarms the shooting renegades by using a rope of solid light to cut their guns in two. Amadou induces a freezing temperature beneath the enemies to allow Takara to disarm them.

Captain Ichimada then approaches the city hall to find her uncle. She kills the six guards posted outside the tower's base with a single concussive slice, then flies up to the balcony. Corporal Keita and Lieutenant Yamashita support her entry into the twenty-five-story tower. Though they would like to accompany their captain in the building, she instructs them to remain on the tower's balcony. She wants to meet her uncle one last time alone. Because he sent most of his protection out, the former prime minister's five remaining guards are all that stand between him and his niece.

The first guard to meet his end at his niece's hand is thrown out of a window to his doom. The second attempts to shoot the captain, only to have his shot deflected back into his head, while the third has his neck snapped like a wishbone without the captain even touching him. The fourth is torn apart molecule by molecule. As the last to fall, Toshiki's second-in-command tries to reason with her. She places a reassuring left hand on his shoulder before knocking his head off his shoulders with an aggressive uppercut.

Standing at the end of the corridor with no open exit, Prince Toshiki talks about the deal they made. He put his most insane renegade in the spotlight to make the grand councilor look weak. Rika promised her uncle that he would return to his former position of power in return for advancing her goals. She also promised that they would find out what happened to King Ito. Since his niece has dispatched all witnesses to his duplicitous nature as he expected, he asks where his escape route is.

He receives his answer when Rika unsheathes her knife to slowly stalk toward him. As she approaches, she taps the knife against the wall to sound *ting, ting, ting*. Her dear uncle, who is not presenting himself as a threat, pleads for mercy to the silent captain approaching him with an insatiable bloodlust. A wide smile on her face remains as she continues to tap the knife, *ting, ting, ting*. In the middle of his final plea, he realizes the truth behind their agreement. Since his demise is an absolute necessity to her goal, she drags the knife across the wall before viciously cutting him down.

The only ones who could lay their eyes on the events that transpired inside the tower are dead. Corporal Keita observes the army's victory over the renegades below; Lieutenant Yamashita looks upon the battlefield with pride and joy. They and the Ark Strikers have received high praise and awards for their actions. As the officer responsible for leading this company of krydian soldiers, Captain Rika Ichimada is thrust into the spotlight as the nation's hero. She is now more loved than when she was a princess living in the pristine palace.

When speaking with the media, one independent journalist questions how positive the ultimate outcome of this action will be. Although Phantom Sword is without its leader, it remains to be a threat. Grand Councilor Keita assures them that the military's direct control of the capital will only last as long as the Phantom Crisis. Amadou and Fatouma ponder the question with a need to find answers. The day after the mission, they decide to speak with the journalist after sneaking around the security. Ji Yong reminds them about rogue elements in the country's top arms company working with Phantom Sword.

Ji questioned how military-grade weapons disappeared from the top manufacturer's warehouses. A whistleblower within Icon Tech told him that 56 million Rimars in off-the-books funding was provided to Phantom Sword after Catcher was arrested. Fatouma asks Ji why this would happen, only to be shocked by what he told him next. Rogue soldiers of the Army of Rosellon were present at the warehouse that was missing three crates of supplies when they were given to Phantom Sword. The whistleblower disappeared before he could acquire any physical evidence to provide to the grand councilor.

Aminata then speaks with her siblings about Ji's report. She is sickened to know that those she expected to be protectors would be so heinously underhanded. While Fatouma thinks it could be a small number of officers that could be neutralized, Aminata fears the situation is much worse. It has become clear that soldiers in her very unit might also be involved in this conspiracy. The bonds she has forged with them are now thrown into question.

Following her productive meeting with the grand councilor, Ryoko meets with her daughter. Rika is glad that everything is progressing so well. Ryoko asks her if she honestly believes that now is the right time and if she has prepared for all outcomes. She reminds her mother that she has remained fully determined to execute her plan to take her throne since her father's idiocy took it away from her. She then tells her mother that she has made it a good practice to be versatile with every major variable.

Ryoko says with sincerity, "Such a shame you had to be rid of him."

Feeling the combat knife she used to kill her uncle in her utility belt, Rika says, "It's a shame he wasn't a better father." They then reflect on how King Ito was so self-indulgent that he neglected his wife and daughters. Even when she was a little girl, he rarely ever took the time to be a father to her. Ryoko, on the other hand, always made sure her daughter knew she was loved. He was once a charming man, but she grew to hate her husband over the years for neglecting his responsibilities to his family and driving Emiko and Kagami away.

Ryoko was livid at her husband's sheer arrogance and idiocy. Before he could leave the palace, Rika used the knife she transformed when her powers awakened to stab him to death. Though the queen was slightly thrown off by her daughter's ferocity, she still aided her in getting rid of any evidence of his death. Upon reflecting on what motivated her at that time, Ryoko then asks her daughter what drives her current actions. In response, Rika arduously states,

> I want to create peace.
> A peace that will be in my image.
> I see the conflict in our society, and it is my guiding hand that must shape the harmony it needs.
> The throne was my chance to do just that.
> Since that idiot cost me what I was to inherit, it was necessary for him to die.
> Even though he was an embarrassing excuse for a father, my murder of him does not mean I am good.

His neglect does not motivate who I have
become.
I am the evil the people need!
I will be their empress!

Rika has graciously reminded her mother that she will stop
at nothing to reclaim her lost throne. Before they part ways, Rika
thanks her mother for inspiring her and always letting her know of
her value. As she leaves to arrange one last bit of business to further
her ambition, Ryoko says to her daughter, "Anything for you, my
sunshine."

8

Enemy or Friend?

AMINATA, TAKARA, TLALLI, AND XOCHITL HEAD BACK to Ruby's Café to celebrate the end of Toshiki Ichimada. Aminata enjoys a bowl of soup while her best friend chows down on a bowl of Somen noodles, and the Valiente sisters eat delicious red leaf lettuce pastrami sandwiches with cranberry jelly. Aminata believes that since the crisis is drawing down, she might pursue university education. Xochitl tells her, "Don't go thinking our problems end with Toshiki. Even we could wind up being the problem."

Takara says, "Having amazing powers is nice, but all this fighting can wear down on a girl," in response.

Aminata confidently states, "I joined the army so I could put an end to that evil prince, and now he is no more. I can wash all my cares away."

Tlalli responds, "Not before you and I have a rematch." Takara is puzzled at her comrade's desire to fight after a grueling hard-fought victory.

Suddenly, their conversation is interrupted by a loud crash. A soldier has taken it upon himself to break a table when the waiter told him he could not have his meal with a free extra side. He insults the waiter and the restaurant in his rude tirade. Tlalli cuts him off with a backhand slap to knock him to the ground. After giving him a quick lesson in manners, she says, "I thought soldiers were supposed to be tough."

The whiny coward tells the three women to wait until General Vetrov hears about Tlalli assaulting a fellow soldier. Aminata graciously reminds him she is the grand councilor's daughter. After he excuses himself from the vicinity, Takara says, "Guess he thought martial law meant he could do whatever he wanted." She reconstructs the table, then apologizes to the waiter for having to put up that unwarranted behavior from one of the troops. Tlalli remarks that her point has been made better than she can say it.

The general severely punishes the bratty subordinate for his inconsiderate actions by making him work to compensate for breaking the table. The women grow concerned that the increasing power of the military could breed problems worse than this. Darion says it is good that they as protectors mean well when Aminata tells him about the experience. Xochitl says, "That guy said he was telling Vetrov. I think he's not a big fan of your father."

Determined to stop who is plotting against her father, Aminata sets out to find answers. She continues to act naturally around her fellow soldiers while trying to find out who is loyal and who is rogue. The heavily armed guards at the barracks and around the palace could also possibly be rogue. Darion, Takara, and Tlalli do not suspect anything about who is concocting this plot.

After telling her parents the news, her father lets her know that he cannot act on it without risk. Adama knows that the plotters could initiate their plan immediately if he made his move without neutralizing the possible conspirators. Grand Councilor Keita suspects it could be General Ivan Vetrov as he was told earlier. Aminata finds it hard to believe that he would do something that heinous. As reported by Major General Ryoko Ichimada, one of the soldiers present at the meeting with Phantom Sword in that warehouse reported directly to General Vetrov.

When Aminata sets off to find answers at the base, Lieutenant Yamashita is waiting there to brief the unit. At seven in the night, just an hour after she left the palace, Aminata arrives just in time to ready herself for her next mission. While Aminata is cooling her nerves, she is told that they must apprehend a rogue officer. The target is none other than General Ivan Vetrov. Known for perceiving

His Eminence to be weak, he is suspected of planning to act on his dissenting opinion.

Since the grand councilor knows the fifty-six-year-old general likes to go to sleep at nine, he has ordered them to stealthily apprehend him before his guards can be alerted. Torn between his love for his father and the oath he took as a soldier, Maxim is ordered to stay put by the captain. Even though they know they have no choice but to follow their orders, Aminata and Darion hate to break their friend's heart. They proceed to the general's house to find that it is guarded against intrusion and disruption to his sleep.

Lieutenant Yamashita uses sound replication to draw the guards away long enough for her and Takara to enter. Once inside, they signal for the troops surrounding the area to neutralize the guards outside. Just as it seems their task is complete in the easiest manner, they are surprised to find that the general has disappeared. An alarm sounds throughout the base to signal a manhunt for the general. Accused of plotting a coup, the most respected officer in the army is now a wanted man.

Ivan moves as quickly as he can without breathing heavily or saying a single word. He hopes his son is nearby to help him when he spots a running soldier in his path to gate 3. Lieutenant Yamashita utilizes sound detection in her hunt as she rushes to gate 3 after detecting something unusual. Suddenly, the soldier in Ivan's path stops upon hearing a noise. He hides and holds his breath as the silhouetted soldier approaches him.

He grows ever more frightened hearing the footsteps get closer until he hears a familiar voice say, "General Vetrov." Ivan is relieved to see his son's best friend, Jack Killdeer, aid in his escape. Unbeknownst to the rest of the army, Jack delivered the warning to him forty-five minutes before the operation to capture him began. Ivan is told to meet his son at the train station to Akamot. Zynda, eager to catch the general, realizes he has left the base and orders Aminata and Darion to venture off base.

At the train station, the general on the run grabs the supplies left by Vissarion to board. Aminata and Darion arrive to spot him getting his ticket. Though her orders are concrete, she is not sure on what to do due to the arbitrary nature of the operation. Darion thinks if General Vetrov is as duplicitous as they are led to believe, stopping him there would put an end to their trouble. Instead of aggressively arresting him as their superiors would desire, they allow him to disappear onto the train.

Speaking into her watch, Aminata tells the lieutenant their target was gone when they got there. Darion says, "You know they are not going to be happy with us."

His comrade responds, "All my problems just disappeared to another country, and I don't have to upset a friend."

The lieutenant is furious to have been too late to capture her target, but her superiors are pleased. As General Vetrov is suspected of trying to overthrow the grand councilor, Ryoko Ichimada succeeds him as secretary of the Security Council. The time has come.

9

A Crown Cold No More!

THERE IS CALM AND EASE AT THE palace and at the base now that Aminata believes the biggest threat to her family is no longer a problem. She made plans to go to the bowling alley with Darion. She says to Darion, "After taking on all these intense missions, we deserve a break." After agreeing not to use their powers to cheat, they begin playing. Aminata displays her strong cocky side when she is trouncing Darion 75–23.

Darion starts adjusting his form when he overhears a familiar voice shout, "Yeah," with a strike. The two look over to see Amadou and Takara also bowling two lanes over. Bewildered for a second, Aminata then realizes it was her brother who Takara was mentioning when they got to Violet View. After finishing their game, Aminata walks over to surprise her brother and best friend. Upon seeing her best friend, their dialogue is as follows:

> Takara: Oh, guess I forgot to tell you I was dating
> your brother.
> Aminata: I'm your best friend, and you forgot to
> tell me you're dating my brother?
> Takara: I didn't have the time. You know we've
> been busy.
> Aminata: How long have you been dating?

> Takara: After Autumn Green. I started liking
> him after we rescued him from that psycho,
> Malicine.
> Aminata: I figured you two were going to get
> together eventually.

As the pair continue their talk, Darion and Amadou discuss how to help each other. Amadou suggests to his best friend that he take his sister to the art museum. At the end of their game, it is Amadou who scores the highest at 234. Having had their fun, they go their respective separate ways to connect elsewhere. Amadou and Takara head to the park, while Darion and Aminata go to the art museum as suggested.

There, Aminata falls head over heels for the expressions of creative passion. Darion finds himself growing emotionally attached to the beauty before his eyes. All around them is a creation made with love, and it all feels serene in the moment when Aminata gets a call from her sister. Eager to resume her time with Darion, Aminata is disappointed when she is told she must get back to the palace immediately. With what seems to be no choice but to cut her evening short, she tells him that she had fun and would love to do this again.

Once she arrives at the palace, she is greeted by her sister. Fatouma escorts her to the garden where she also meets her brother. They ask what could be so urgent as to disrupt their evenings. Fatouma tells them she was getting Mom's flowers when she stumbled upon a metal piece of an Icon Tech crate. Using energy detection, Aminata deduces that it is too recent to be connected to General Vetrov's alleged plot.

Even though Catcher was arrested, Aminata believes it is necessary to investigate his company. As her family members are the only people she can completely trust, her brother and sister help her sneak into the company's headquarters to find answers. At Icon Tech's office tower, Aminata discovers that Tyson Catcher was innocent when she sees video and audio files that show he was trying to stop the flow of supplies from the company into Phantom Sword as he said he was. Since he had been telling the truth, someone had to have a personal stake in his removal. The immediate suspect is no one other than his successor, Dr. Isai Valeka Orozco.

Dr. Orozco was working on several projects revolving around krydium that Catcher refused to fund. Catcher shunned his idea to use krydium in their advanced weapon systems. An armored suit powered by krydium was firmly rejected. Lastly was a project focused on neutralizing the effect of krydium on a person's body. As a result of the former king's disastrous violent attempt to get complete control of the substance, the company could not do much about it.

The renegade army provided the scorned scientist with valuable resources for his desires until he arrogantly threatened to reveal their locations for more funding. With Dr. Orozco at the head of the company, he could have full reign over Icon Tech's projects with military oversight. With this connection fully made, Aminata has a horrific realization. The chaos caused by Phantom Sword presented a pretext for the army to hold power for themselves. This is especially true with Dr. Orozco in particular since he did not know of the soldiers present at that meeting with Phantom Sword.

It was the one rogue soldier that drew suspicion toward General Vetrov. Aminata's eavesdropping is cut short by her brother via silent call. She is unable to leave back through the way she came while her siblings must leave the premises as security approaches. Although no alarms are triggered, Aminata tells them to meet her back at the palace. She proceeds to make her escape through the warehouse.

It is at this warehouse where those three crates of supplies were stolen. Using her ergokinetic abilities, she finds and interrogates the workers Darion overheard. They tell her that they moved those supplies to Phantom Sword on Dr. Orozco's orders. Showing up in time to test his new battle armor, Dr. Orozco is pleased to see a powerful soldier he can test his gear with. A hard battle ensues between the ergokinetic youngster and the mad scientist.

Isai says, "My work will bring wonders to the world," as he begins his battle. Aminata's training and skill keep him at bay. She causes him to run into one of the tanks to leave his power source to be exploited. After disabling the armor by taking out the krydium in his back, she asks him who his contact was. Applying more pressure in her interrogation, he tells her, "That fool never gave genius the time of day, but she has vision." This makes it clear that he was supplying Phantom Sword for his own benefit and receiving greater help.

The treacherous doctor is in a prime position to be prosecuted for working with such devious characters. Before Aminata can start taking him to the authorities, she feels the ground shake. The defeated high executive tells her, "I'm afraid you no longer have your father's protection." Without a second thought, Aminata races as fast as she can to Parliament where her father is set to attend the emergency session. Her family is in grave danger, and the only thought on her mind is their safety.

While racing through the city, Aminata sees a thick cloud of smoke rising from where the capitol complex should be. The capitol complex has been reduced to scorching rubble during the emergency session of Parliament. Aminata treads through the smoldering remains of the once-mighty structure to search for her father. Not one of the 665 members of Parliament is seen alive. The young soldier is relieved to see emergency services arrive shortly after.

Not finding him, she asks a guard what happened to her father. In response, he tells her that he has been arrested. Captain Ichimada, to Corporal Keita's displeasure, arrested the grand councilor on suspicion of mass murder. His daughter, knowing this cannot be true, comes to realize that her captain's intentions were far from virtuous. With a violent coup underway, she immediately runs home the fastest she has ever run.

At her home, she is greeted by Lieutenant Yamashita along with the rest of Ark Strikers Unit 380 posted around the palace. She lets her know that the captain would like to see her. All pieces of the puzzle come together for Aminata so that she can see that her captain was the chess master behind the crisis that motivated her to become a soldier. It has all been a twisting road of deceit and treachery from someone she has come to trust.

Inside the palace, she meets Captain Rika Ichimada. It is now fully apparent that her own direct superior was at the heart of the Phantom Crisis. She has had a hand in causing all the major conflicts that have transpired from the assassination attempt on her father, the terror of Malicine, to the framing of General Vetrov. The woman who stands before Aminata is her greatest enemy. Their dialogue is as follows:

> Aminata: No wonder you never gave up your title.
>
> Rika: Ever since I had everything ripped away from me, I did not care who I had to crush to get it back.
>
> Aminata: You just killed hundreds for this. Was Vaughn even my first kill?
>
> Rika: No, he was a dead man the second he thought he could throw my trust away. Thanks for making my arrangement much easier.
>
> Aminata: And my graduation?
>
> Rika: I recommended my uncle to send those so-called assassins. They were never going to succeed.
>
> Aminata: You could've overthrown my father sooner, right?
>
> Rika: Correct. But it was never enough.
>
> Aminata: Enough?
>
> Rika: For me to simply take power like a common coup plotter would be unremarkable. The people had to believe in me.
>
> Aminata: You can sit there and act like you're above us, but you are nothing but a psychotic murderer.
>
> Rika: Yes, but this is how the story will go: your father manipulated the army into targeting his rivals and killed Parliament in an effort to attain absolute power until I, the gracious heroine, saved the people from his insanity.

Aminata: You really think anybody's going to believe that?

Rika: They already do. Here's how the story can end: I, the kind empress, allowed you and your family to live happy lives with my protection.

Aminata: Rika.

Rika: Yes.

Aminata: I am not your pawn!

In the palace they have both called home, Aminata will not allow this obscene treachery to prevail. Determined to put an end to the captain's scheme, she furiously charges at her superior officer with her weapons drawn and personal energy amplified. Holding nothing back, she puts her all into stopping her adversary. In her effort, she utilizes her most powerful offensive techniques. She refuses to lose, and she will not back down!

Expending energy by the second, Aminata realizes her captain's deceit also extended to her own physical abilities as a krydian. Rika had been keeping the full extent of her strength, speed, and durability a secret. Her skill in combat combined with her ability to fly and interact with solid objects from a distance were only a minuscule fraction of her prowess. She has used telekinesis to improve her disposition to the point where no basic attack could hurt her. With her immense power of mind over matter, she phases through the walls, then causes Aminata to trudge through the floor like it was mud. Whatever solid matter she must quickly go through can be reconstructed as easily as it is destroyed.

The young corporal uses her speed to evade her captain's attacks with haste. The field she creates around her keeps her from taking the full force of Rika's concussive blasts and cuts. Her last attack unfortunately brings her within Captain Ichimada's reach. Now in the grasp of her enemy, she is punched into the air, pulled back, and slammed. With the fight all but won, Rika says to Aminata, "Can you not see what you can accomplish under my guiding hand?"

Beaten and bloodied, Aminata begins to pass out. She struggles to stand in defeat to see her archnemesis standing in front of her with the knife she used to kill her father and uncle. Rika approaches to deal with the killing strike, then suddenly, Aminata disappears in the blink of an eye. Takara, who was watching out of sight of the captain and her lieutenant, witnesses the depth of her deceit be revealed. Since she cannot hurt Rika, the only action she can take is to save Aminata with her hyper-accelerated speed. As the fastest soldier, Takara runs far away from her former superior's reach.

The Keita family is left with no choice but to escape, separate, and hide. Now forcibly deposed, Adama Keita disappears along with his wife. Rika does not feel too dissatisfied that her enemy was rescued from her grasp. She has trusted the task of finding her rebellious subordinates with her right-hand woman, Lieutenant Zynda Yamashita. Since Aminata is the only one she knows who can physically challenge her, she wants her to be found.

There is now no obstacle that stands in the way of her goal. The Ark Strikers affirm their loyalty to their captain. They do not know what was revealed inside the palace due to their orders to stand guard outside. While most are confident in their faith, Ace and Tlalli are hesitant because of the strong bonds they forged with them.

It is the next day on the thirty-first of October when Army Captain Rika Ichimada makes her stunning announcement to the people of Rosellon. The destruction of the capitol complex and mass murder of Parliament have prompted her to take drastic measures. With the grand councilor accused of manipulating the crisis to anoint himself with more power, she proclaims herself to be Rosellon's new leader. As state authority is now at her disposal, she intends to restore the monarchy and finally take her crown. Out of the fear stoked by the crisis, she is granted respect from the population.

For Rika, this is the culmination of five long years of treachery, manipulation, and development. With the army under her command and the country under her control, she is victorious. Her deception and scheming over the years have worked. Not only does she carry the legitimacy of being an army officer, a princess, and now the leader, but the people believe in her. She is supreme!

For Aminata, this is a defeat that will change her life forever. No longer is she the daughter of the most powerful man in the country. The challenges she must face are far greater than ever before. As she clings on to life, her friend runs as fast as she can to get her to safety. They are now recognized as renegades.

Takara is so immensely desperate to find medical attention for her best friend that she runs to Akamot. She meets border guards to request asylum and aid for Aminata. Upon approval, Takara defects to the People's Army of Akamot and accompanies her friend to the hospital. The doctors tell her that Aminata is in a coma after being defeated. All is dire for Takara, with her best friend close to death, her comrades betraying her, and her enemies victorious.

Aminata wakes up in a hospital bed to see Takara and Darion in front of her. They are relieved that she has recovered from her fight. After embracing them, she looks over to notice something strange in a nurse's hand. The nurse is holding a two-hundred-Rimar banknote with Rika smiling on it. Questioning why something like this would even exist, Darion tells her that it has been five months since it happened. With Chairman Tokala's hospitality in Akamot, they have been doing what they can for Aminata's safety and their loved ones back home.

Aminata exclaims, "EMPRESS?" with shock as she holds the shameful piece of money in her hand. She turns to the television in front of her to see the media reporting on the coronation of the empress. With the Ark Strikers and Prime Minister Morvolio Moretti at her side, Rika is crowned by her mother as the empress of Rosellon in the Palace of the Empire. She walks to the balcony to address the crowd. Her address is as follows:

> People of Rosellon, you have endured chaos, betrayal, and fear.
> As your empress, I will protect you.
> Many died so that we may succeed.
> Under my guiding hand, you will know only peace and prosperity!

Anyone who dares to challenge that will suffer!

With my power as a krydian, I am unstoppable, and so shall you.

This is a victory I have achieved for you!

Long live the Empire of Rosellon!

The crowd chants her name in appreciation for their ruler. The anchorman finishes his report with a closing remark, "Long reign the empress! Long live Rika." Greatly discomforted, Takara tells her that nobody could stop her. Since seizing power, she has gained a reputation for being personally involved in battles. As Phantom Sword has been defeated with no significant remnants left, Rika is admired as the "triumphant empress."

Unbroken by what transpired five months ago, Aminata feels rage that she has never felt before. She underestimated the evil that was in front of her because she believed she could win without surrendering her innocence. Though her physical wounds have healed, the pain of failure is ever present. Her enemy must face justice for her deceit and heartless nature. Reuniting with her family and finding her happiness again are what drives her determination. She hates to hear the crowd chant, "Rika, Rika, Rika," but she still has a chance to fight.

About the Author

GROWING UP IN A SMALL FISHING TOWN in the South, Tyler Christian Williams had a very active imagination. He had an appreciation for action-oriented stories with compelling characters. As he grew, Tyler developed a skill for critiquing stories in film, television, and gaming. Out of this tendency to critique, he acquired a sense of what makes a good story. After attaining his degree in political science, he compiled his thoughts on his favorite media and decided to make a story of his own. In his study of superhuman abilities and story structure, his creative process was influenced by some of the greatest science fiction and shonen anime. He imagined a diverse group of characters who develop with one another and their environment. In this novella, he focuses on characters wielding superhuman abilities and their actions that transform the plot.